SOME SWAHILI WORDS

Cheka
to joke

Lulu
pearl, precious

Muwa
sugar cane

Nzee
old

Nzuri
good, beautiful

Pudini
caramel pudding

Sukari
sugar

Mayai
eggs

Pamba
cotton

DISNEY'S

THE
LION KING

HOW TRUE, ZAZU?

by Leslie McGuire

Illustrations by Laureen Burger
Brooks & Rachelle Campbell
David Pacheco
Denise Shimabukuro

Produced by Mega-Books, Inc. Design and art direction by Michaelis/Carpelis Design Assoc., Inc.
Printed in the United States of America.

Grolier Books

ISBN: 0-7172-8349-6

CHAPTER

hy is the sky blue?" asked Kopa.

Zazu smiled. "The earth liked that color so much, it put blue all over the sky to look at." Zazu was steward to Kopa's father, Simba, the Lion King. He was baby-sitting Kopa while his mother, Nala, was hunting and Simba was taking a nap.

"And why do trees grow so tall?" asked Kopa.

"Because trees like the flavor of air that's way up high." Zazu could see a long morning of questions from Kopa. They were resting on Pride Rock, which overlooked the vast grasslands all the way to the blue hills.

"And why do you fly so far around the Pride Lands?" asked Kopa.

"I fly everywhere so I can see everything and report to your father." Zazu stared at the silver Zuberi River, which meandered across the plain. It would be wonderful to fly to Zulu Falls right now, he thought.

"But why?"

"Because it's important, and he knows I'll tell him the truth about what is going on in the Pride Lands." Yes, a cold drink of water at Zulu Falls would be marvelous.

"But why?" asked Kopa.

Zazu took a deep breath. No Zulu Falls for him this morning. Kopa would never let him go. But these questions had gone on for long enough. From now on, he'd do all the talking.

"Let me tell you a story," said Zazu with a smile.

"I love stories," said Kopa. "Is there a big ugly beast with three horns and sharp teeth in it?"

"As a matter of fact, there is, sort of."

Kopa sat up. "I'm all ears," he said. He had heard his mother say that to Simba. It made him feel grown up to say it to Zazu.

Zazu preened his feathers, cleared his throat, and began to speak.

"News gathering is a family tradition for me," he said. "My mother, Zuzu, was the steward to your great-grandfather, Ahadi. When I was still a fledgling, she began to train me to take her place with Ahadi's son, Mufasa, when he became the Lion King." Zazu puffed out his feathers. The hot sun felt good.

"Mufasa's son, Simba—your father—was next in line to be the Lion King. But Mufasa's evil brother, Scar, wanted to be king himself. Scar and his hyena cronies killed Mufasa, and Scar convinced Simba that he had caused his father's death.

Simba ran away to a distant jungle to forget what he thought he had done. As you might expect, Scar was a bad ruler, and your mother, Nala, went on a journey to look for help. In her hunt, she found Simba and told him he had to return to the Pride Lands and take his rightful place as Lion King."

Kopa nodded seriously. He had heard this story before. "And then my father defeated Scar and became the new Lion King," he said.

"All this happened long ago, before you were born," said Zazu. "The story I am going to tell you took place before your father was born. Mufasa had just become the Lion King."

"Is Uncle Scar in the story?"

"No, he was spending most of his time away from Pride Rock because he could not bear to see his brother rule the Pride Lands."

"I'll bet he was hanging with the hyenas, right?"

Zazu nodded. "As I said, this was a long time ago, and Mufasa was busy learning how to rule. He wasn't giving much thought to his brother then."

"Is that when you became Mufasa's steward?"

"When my mother saw what a fine ruler Mufasa was, she decided it was time for her to retire so she could travel. Mufasa made me his steward in her place. Mama pecked me on the beak and flew off to follow the Zuberi River to its source. I was on my own, but she had trained me well—perhaps too well. I reported everything I observed to Mufasa, which was a mistake."

"What's wrong with that?" asked Kopa.

"It's not necessary to report every little thing. But I had a hard time telling the difference between what was important and what was petty. I tried to give Mufasa all the information I could so that bad things wouldn't happen."

"But why do bad things happen?"

"Everything we do makes something happen. We have to think about others around us," said Zazu. "If you pull up a bush on the plain, you might be pulling up some little creature's house. Or if you tell someone there's no danger when there is, he might get hurt."

"I get it!" said Kopa. "You should be careful about what you do and say."

"Right!" said Zazu. "But I was *so* worried somebody might get hurt, I kept poking my nose into everyone's business. And it kept getting me into trouble."

"What kind of trouble?"

"Well, once, for instance, I overheard two of the ostriches talking about beating another ostrich. I didn't like the sound of that, so I told Mufasa. He went right over to those ostriches to find out what was going on. It turned out they were talking about beating another ostrich in a kicking contest. Ostriches are fine kickers."

"So, how do you keep from making that kind of mistake?" asked Kopa.

"You have to check out the situation carefully so that you have a clear idea of what is happening," Zazu said. "I remember my first summer in particular, when my reporting got out of hand and terrible things happened. It was a lesson from which we all learned a great deal."

CHAPTER 2

The morning sun shone down on the animals gathering at the water hole. Nzee, an antelope, stood off to one side, staring into the distance. Her daughter, Nzuri, was nearby, munching on grass.

"What's the matter?" asked Pembe the elephant, who was on her way to the water hole with her two children, Lulu and Cheka. "Why aren't you drinking?"

"Oh, it's that nosy Zazu," answered Nzee. "It's terrible the way he reports everything we do to Mufasa. I told little Nzuri that the grass was better on the east side of the water hole, and Zazu went and told Mufasa that I didn't like the grass on the west side. Then Mufasa came by and asked me what was wrong with the grass!"

"I know what you mean," said Pembe. "You can't do anything without that flying newspaper telling the whole world about it."

Muwa, a zebra, joined the group with her son, Sukari. He nodded and said, "And then we get into trouble."

"What kind of trouble?" asked Muwa. "What have you been up to?"

"All we were doing was having a little fun yesterday," said Sukari.

Cheka spoke up. "Yeah, what's with Zazu anyway? Sukari, Lulu, Nzuri, and I were chasing the baby ostriches, and the next thing we know, Mufasa comes running up and tells us to stop being mean to them."

"Well, Zazu was only doing his job," said Pembe. "He has to keep the king informed."

"If you ask me, he's overdoing it," said Sukari.

"We've got to do something about that bird," said Nzee. "I'm afraid to open my mouth."

"We could give Zazu wrong information," said Cheka. "That way, he'd get in trouble with Mufasa."

"That sounds like fun," said Nzuri.

"No, it doesn't," said Nzee. She sighed. "You children will have to think of better games to play. Pembe, Muwa, and I will discuss this further."

"I think we should call a council of the animals," said Pembe.

"Do we have to include the ostriches?" asked Muwa. "They have such a short attention span."

The adult animals went off to talk and graze a short distance from the water hole. The young ones stayed and frolicked in the water. Cheka filled his trunk and splashed the others. Then he motioned to them to gather around.

"Listen, you guys, I've made up a game for us to play. It's called get-Zazu."

"But," said Lulu, "Mama told us—"

"Give me a break, Lulu," Cheka said. "Since when do we wait for adults to do anything? They don't want us to have any fun."

"I'm with you, Cheka," said Nzuri. "I'm really tired of Zazu's tattletale ways. How do you play get-Zazu?"

Cheka looked around. "We're going to make up stories."

"I love stories," said Lulu. "But I don't want anyone to get hurt."

"Aw, come on," said Sukari. "We're not going to hurt anyone."

"Don't worry, Lulu. It'll be fun," said Nzuri.

"Why don't we pretend a terrible beast is sneaking around the Pride Lands!" said Cheka. "We can start a rumor about it. Zazu is sure to tell Mufasa. But there won't be any beast at all!"

Sukari laughed and began chasing

Nzuri in a circle. "Get Zazu!" he cried.

When they quieted down, Lulu said, "We can get the other animals to start talking about the beast. You know how everyone loves to gossip."

"Cool!" said Sukari.

"I like this idea," Nzuri said. "The flying newspaper will go straight to Mufasa with a false alarm." She giggled.

"Let's get the baby ostriches in on this," said Cheka. "They're always squawking and running around. They'll get everybody really worried!"

Cheka filled his trunk and sprayed the others again.

"Get Zazu!" Sukari cried.

They all laughed.

Pudini, the mother of two young ostriches, overheard Cheka's plan. Children have no idea what trouble lies can cause, she thought. She had to find her babies and warn them about the dangers of crying wolf. But then a fat, juicy bug ran by, and she forgot all about it.

CHAPTER

N zuri, Lulu, Cheka, and Sukari met the ostrich babies near the water hole the next day and told them how to play get-Zazu.

"So all we have to do is wander around and ask everyone if they've seen or heard a strange beast in the Pride Lands?" asked Mayai.

"Why should we do that?" asked his sister, Pamba.

"Because we want everyone to start worrying," said Lulu.

"If we get everyone spooked about the beast, Zazu will hear about it and report it to Mufasa. Zazu will look silly for reporting it," explained Sukari.

"Oh, this is going to be such fun," said Mayai.

"Are you sure we should do this?" asked Pamba.

"Oh, Pamba, you're such a scaredy-cat. This will be fun," said Mayai.

"Don't worry. It'll be a hoot to watch Zazu get yelled at by Mufasa," said Nzuri. Those ostriches are so silly they've already forgotten how we chased them the other day, she thought.

Mayai and Pamba went in different directions and asked all the animals they met whether they'd heard about the strange beast wandering in the Pride Lands. None of them knew of the beast, but they said they'd keep their eyes and ears open.

Meanwhile, Zazu was giving Mufasa his morning report.

"We have a little problem with the springboks, sire. I really wish you would talk to them about their springing. They

"Where exactly did you talk to him?" asked Zazu.

"Down at the water hole."

"What did he say about this strange creature?" asked Zazu.

"He said he'd heard it made gurgling sounds and that it had three horns and a big ugly nose!" exclaimed the gazelle.

"Hmmm. I'd better go down there and find out about this!" said Zazu.

He headed straight for the water hole. There he found Nzuri and some other young antelopes drinking water.

"Has anyone seen or heard a beast wandering around the Pride Lands?" asked Zazu.

"I thought I saw something strange in the forest near the river," said Nzuri.

"What did it look like, little one?" asked Zazu. "Did it have three horns and a big ugly nose?"

Nzuri nodded. "Well, uh, yes . . . er . . . um, that's it! Three horns and a big ugly nose."

"And did it make a strange gurgling sound?" asked Zazu.

"I didn't hear anything," said Nzuri, looking down at her hooves. "It was too far away. But it was horrible-looking."

"Are you sure?" asked Zazu.

"Oh, yes!" said Nzuri. "It had long, sharp teeth too." The more she talked about the beast, the bigger and uglier it became.

"Very upsetting! This has to be reported to the king right away!" said Zazu in his most official manner. He flew off to tell Mufasa about the menace.

Mufasa had just come back from talking to the springboks and visiting his mate, Sarabi. Zazu flew up and breathlessly told him about the beast.

"I'd better have a look," said Mufasa. "This kind of talk could start a panic."

"Yes, sire. I agree completely," said Zazu.

"An animal like that might be dangerous," said Mufasa.

"Oh, very dangerous, sire. I will fly far and wide to help with the search!" said Zazu.

So Mufasa went off to look for the beast. First he talked to Boma, the Cape buffalo. Boma was nervous because an elephant had told him about the beast. He hadn't seen anything yet, but if an elephant was scared, he was scared too.

Mufasa searched for the beast all day. The cheetahs told him they hadn't seen the beast, only heard about it from some little ostriches.

As darkness fell over the Pride Lands, Mufasa had no choice but to stop searching. He wondered if Zazu had any more news. Mufasa knew he wouldn't sleep well until the mystery of the beast was solved.

CHAPTER 4

The next morning, the young animals gathered at the water hole. Sukari didn't think the beast story had worked. "Mufasa searched hard, but he didn't blame Zazu for the wild-beast chase," he said. Nzuri, the elephants, and the little ostriches agreed with him.

"How can we fool Zazu this time?" asked Cheka.

"Maybe we should pretend there's another strange beast wandering all over the Pride Lands," said Mayai. He'd enjoyed running around and telling everyone the false news.

"Nah, let's do something different," said Pamba.

"How about making wild noises in the night?" asked Lulu.

"That's not different enough," said Nzuri.

"Let's see," said Cheka. "Why don't we report someone missing?"

"That's a good one," exclaimed Lulu.

"Okay. We'll tell Zazu that Mayai is missing," said Cheka. He turned to Mayai. "You get on Lulu's back and hide with her in the forest near the river."

"Oh, boy!" cried Mayai. Lulu knelt down, and Mayai ran and jumped onto her back.

"This will be fun," said Sukari, laughing as Lulu and Mayai trotted off to the river.

A short while later, Zazu was flying over the water hole when he saw the young animals waving for him to come down. The minute he landed, Pamba ran up to him, fluttering her wings.

"Oh, Zazu, I haven't seen my brother, Mayai, for hours! Maybe the strange beast caught him!"

"Where did you last see him?" asked Zazu.

"Well, we were playing hide-the-feather in the trees near Five Stones. I went off to hide the feather, and when I came back, he was gone!" cried Pamba.

"All right, take it easy, Pamba. We'll find him," said Zazu.

"Don't tell my mother yet. She'll be so worried. Promise?"

"Sometimes it's better if bad news waits until it can become no news," said Zazu. He flew off and told Mufasa about Mayai. "Perhaps the beast caught him!" he finished.

Mufasa was the best tracker in the Pride Lands, and he hunted everywhere. He ran to Five Stones while Zazu flew overhead. He and Zazu looked behind each of the Five Stones. They found no trace of Mayai or the beast. They checked the elephant graveyard, even though it was forbidden. Then they went to the river.

"Let's search the forest," Mufasa said.

Zazu nodded. He heard a rustling. "Look!" he cried.

Lulu and Mayai were coming out from the trees as if nothing were wrong.

"Where have you been?" asked Mufasa. "Zazu heard Mayai was lost. We thought the beast had caught him!"

"He wasn't lost, sire," said Lulu. "We were playing in the forest."

"I'm glad to hear that. It must have been a mistake," said Mufasa.

"But your sister—" began Zazu.

Mayai laughed. "Pamba's an airhead."

Zazu realized there was some truth in Mayai's statement. Ostriches were known for getting ruffled over nothing. He'd made a mistake trusting someone who was not reliable. "I must go, sire," he

told Mufasa and then flew off.

Although he was annoyed, Mufasa said nothing. When he got back to the water hole, he heard the animals calling Zazu the "flying false alarm" and talking about his mistakes. Mufasa shook his head and continued on his way back to Pride Rock.

"This is more like it," said Sukari, staring after Mufasa.

"Yeah, Zazu is starting to look like the silly loudspeaker that he is!" Cheka laughed.

"Let's try another trick," said Pamba.

"We can make Zazu believe there's an earthquake," said Lulu. She began to stomp.

Nzuri laughed. "That won't work. He'd see you. Besides, when there's an earthquake, everyone feels it."

Sukari cleared his throat. "I have an excellent idea. Let's tell Zazu that hyenas have grabbed an antelope."

"I'm not sure I like that one," said Nzuri with a shiver. "How about hyenas grabbing a zebra?"

"How about hyenas grabbing a baby wildebeest?" said Sukari.

"Let's go," said Nzuri, and she and the other animals raced off. They found Zazu at the top of an acacia tree, looking worried.

"Zazu! Hyenas have attacked a baby wildebeest," exclaimed Cheka.

"Are you sure? Where?" asked Zazu.

"Over by the river," said Sukari. "One of the gazelles told us."

"When?" asked Zazu.

"Just a few minutes ago!" cried Nzuri. "Please hurry!"

Zazu went straight to Mufasa and told him what he had heard. Mufasa hesitated. Suppose Zazu was wrong again? On the other hand, suppose he was right? There was no time to lose.

They raced to the edge of the river. The wildebeests were calmly grazing.

"No one is missing," said a wildebeest. "We haven't seen the hyenas in ages.

They're always hanging around with your brother, Scar."

"What's going on, Zazu?" asked Mufasa. "This is the third time you've dragged me out on a false alarm!"

"But, sire," mumbled Zazu. "I was only reporting—"

"I understand, Zazu," said Mufasa, stalking back to Pride Rock. "But yesterday, you said there was a beast wandering around. Today, you said one of the little ostriches was missing, and then you told me a baby wildebeest had been attacked by the hyenas. I'm beginning to wonder about your judgment!"

"But, sire—"

"Check your facts!" Mufasa said angrily and broke into a gallop.

"I'm acting like a baby bird," Zazu said to himself. "Three serious mistakes in two days. Am I turning into a hysterical, babbling ninny? What will I do if Mufasa fires me?"

CHAPTER 5

Back at Pride Rock, Mufasa puzzled over why Zazu was making so many mistakes. It was true he often reported petty stories, but they'd always been true. Mufasa thought back over the last two days.

It was odd that Zazu had reported so many crises in such a short time. The last two seemed to involve just the young animals. But what did that prove? It was probably only coincidence.

Meanwhile, Zazu had taken to the skies in an effort to fly away from his dark thoughts. But he couldn't stop thinking, no matter how high he flew.

Where will I go and what will I do? he thought. Without the Pride Lands to watch over, my life will be empty. I'll have time to eat and sleep and fly around looking at the wide world. But life won't have the same meaning.

He zoomed down to Five Stones and circled the grasslands. Zebras, antelopes, and wildebeests were grazing peacefully. The elephants were lumbering along, probably looking for new trees. Boma, the big Cape buffalo, was in his own pool.

The sight of Boma brought back a memory of the time Zazu had spotted a stampede of Cape buffaloes. A storm had been brewing in the distance, which was bad enough. But then he'd seen an immense dust cloud moving toward the Pride Lands and heard the awful thunder of the herd of buffaloes. The hyenas had attacked in large numbers and caused the buffaloes to panic. They were running without any sense of where they were going, and they were heading straight for the Pride Lands.

Zazu remembered how calm and steady Mufasa had been when he'd reported the stampede to him. Mufasa had told him to tell the elders to gather near Pride Rock. He had quickly formed a plan to move the animals to a safe place. We were such a good team, Mufasa and I, Zazu thought.

He caught a thermal and soared.

Or how about the time Mufasa, Sarabi, and I went down to the river to relax for an hour or so. I remember Mufasa saying, "Zazu, why don't you take a break and go play upstream while we go for a wade?"

"Oh, no, sire," I told him. "I should stay and keep a lookout for trouble."

"Give it a rest, Zazu!" he told me. "We will be fine. There's nothing to worry about."

"Yes, I know, sire. I just have a hunch I should keep an eye out for the unexpected."

"Zazu!" Mufasa had bellowed. "Go!"

He had something serious to talk to Sarabi about, and he didn't want my big ears in the area.

Well, I obeyed his command. I mean, you can't push your point too hard with Mufasa. He does have a healthy temper. But after a few minutes, I doubled back. And a good thing too. From my vantage point, I could see a water cobra swimming across the river toward Mufasa and Sarabi.

I yelled, "Mufasa! Sarabi! Behind you! A water snake! Get out of the river!"

They got out just in time. Sarabi, of course, thanked me. Mufasa was somewhat miffed, but he said, "Good job, Zazu!"

Yes, we had some great times together, Zazu thought. He flew on to the west. Maybe he'd pay a visit to his old friend Rafiki, the wise baboon. But then he thought, I don't even know where he is.

CHAPTER 6

Zazu flew low over Zulu Falls. He looked down, hoping he'd see Rafiki gathering plants in the mist. It would be good to talk to his old friend. Perhaps Rafiki could help him.

"Wait a second!" Zazu cried. "What's that black mass?" Zazu flew down for a closer look.

"Omigosh," he cried. A chill ran all the way down his spine and out to his wing tips.

"Holy elephants!" yelled Zazu. "Army ants! Eating everything in their path and heading for the Pride Lands! And they're moving fast!"

Zazu wheeled around and headed for Pride Rock. "I've got to warn everyone!" he cried.

But then he thought, What if no one believes me? He was the joke of the Pride Lands because of his false alarms. But this one wasn't false. He had seen the ants with his own eyes.

"Mufasa will believe me," Zazu said to himself. "He must, or the entire kingdom is in danger. If those ants get to the river and cross it, all will be lost."

Zazu flew straight to Pride Rock, where he found Mufasa and Sarabi.

"Mufasa! Sire! The Pride Lands are in grave danger!" Zazu cried. "Army ants are on the march."

Sarabi gasped. "Not army ants!"

"Is this another of your stories?" Mufasa asked.

"Oh, no, sire! I assure you, it is not!"

"Where did you hear the news?" asked Mufasa.

"I saw the ants with my own eyes,"

said Zazu, his voice trembling.

Mufasa could hear the truth in Zazu's voice. Army ants were definitely not a joke.

"Where are they?" asked Mufasa, rising to his feet.

"Quickly, sire, follow me. They're just on the other side of Zulu Falls," said Zazu.

Zazu flew ahead as Mufasa raced across the grasslands to the river and up to Zulu Falls.

Mufasa crossed the river by jumping from rock to rock, keeping an eye out for the crocodiles. When he reached the other side, he leaped onto the bank and looked around. He saw nothing unusual. He walked to the edge of the forest and tried to listen, but the waterfall was too loud.

Zazu perched in a tree. He watched Mufasa enter the forest and disappear.

"Please be careful, Mufasa! The ants have reached the forest!" Zazu called out.

"Don't worry, Zazu, there is nothing . . . ." Mufasa's voice trailed off.

Zazu didn't like the sound of that. He swooped into the forest to get a closer look.

The bushes were being thrashed about violently.

"Yoicks!" he cried. "Something terrible has happened to Mufasa!"

CHAPTER 7

Mufasa leaped out of the forest, roaring and shaking his head. He clawed at his mane and rubbed his eyes. His head was covered with ants.

"The river! Dive in the river," shouted Zazu. "It's right in front of you, Mufasa! Follow my voice!"

Zazu kept shouting as he flew ahead of Mufasa. Blindly, Mufasa followed Zazu's instructions. Roaring in pain, he crashed into the water. The ants loosened their hold on him, and Mufasa swam to the other side of the river.

"Sire, are you all right?" asked Zazu.

"Yes. I'm fine now," he said, shaking the water out of his mane. "Thank you, Zazu. You saved my life! I couldn't see with all those ants biting me. We must warn the others as fast as we can!"

"I'd help you warn everyone," replied Zazu, "but I don't know whether they'd believe me."

"I'll tell them how you warned me and how you begged me to see the ants for myself, Zazu. You are my most trusted friend," said Mufasa.

"I'm so glad to hear you say that, sire," replied Zazu. "Now let's go!"

Mufasa and Zazu raced back to Pride Rock. Sarabi had told everyone about the army ants, but they weren't sure whether to believe her after she said it was Zazu who had seen them. They were waiting for Mufasa to confirm the story. And he did.

"Zazu and I have seen a fearsome column of ants on the other side of the river," Mufasa said. "They're headed here!"

There was a moment of stunned silence. Then Mufasa spoke again. "Everyone must leave immediately!"

The animals knew what army ants did. In panic, they began running in all directions.

Sarabi stepped to Mufasa's side and asked, "What can I do to help?"

"We must get everyone to move together," said Mufasa. "Zazu! Help me get the animals calmed down."

Mufasa, Sarabi, and Zazu yelled to the elders of the herds to calm their young ones. When the animals were quiet, Mufasa told them to follow Sarabi to the high plains.

Next, Mufasa asked Pembe, Boma, Muwa, Pudini, and Nzee to stay and help him stop the ants.

"But how can we stop millions of ants?" asked Pembe.

"I don't know, but I will find a way. Zazu, you fly ahead and find out what the ants are doing."

"Roger," said Zazu, "I'll keep you posted," and he took to the skies.

"Let's get to the river," Mufasa told the others. His mind was racing. He began to form a plan. He hoped and prayed it would work.

"Now, here is the plan," Mufasa said to his helpers as they ran across the plain. "The boulders at the top of Zulu Falls act as a dam and let only so much water through. We can increase the flow by moving them."

"How can we move such big rocks?" asked Muwa.

"The boulders are held in place by smaller rocks," said Mufasa. "If we move the small ones, the boulders will come loose. The river will do the rest of the work for us."

"But, Mufasa, that could be dangerous," said Pudini.

"That's true, but it's the only way to keep the ants from crossing the river," said Mufasa. "The ants are even more dangerous. We have no choice."

"Well, I'm ready for this fight," said Boma. "My grandparents were taken by them years ago. I have never forgotten that awful attack."

"I'm ready too," added Muwa. "Many of my herd were killed in that same attack."

"I remember my father telling me that sad story when I was young," said Mufasa. "Now we have a chance to keep it from happening again. So let's be as brave and skillful as we can!"

Mufasa's courage and strength gave the other animals heart. They would follow him no matter what happened, and they began to run faster.

By now, Zazu was high over the river and could see the ants. Millions of them marched toward the river. The sound of their jaws crunching was so loud, Zazu could hear it above the roar of the water-fall. And they were headed for the one spot in the river where they could cross—

the spot where Mufasa had crossed by jumping from rock to rock. These same rocks would be the army ants' stepping stones, Zazu knew. If they were not stopped, they would make living bridges of their own bodies, stretching in a thick, black rope from rock to rock till they had reached the Pride Lands. But Zazu was sure they could not succeed if the current was swift and strong enough.

Zazu saw Mufasa and his party reach the river and flew down to report.

"The ants are starting to cross," he said grimly.

"So I see. Keep your eye on them," said Mufasa. "We're going to the top of the falls."

"I'll keep you informed," yelled Zazu, and he flew back over the river with fear in his heart.

CHAPTER

Mufasa led his helpers to a rocky path.

"It's not so steep this way," said Mufasa. "But watch your step!" He guided the group up the final few yards to the boulders.

Muwa, Pudini, and Nzee kicked the small rocks out from under the large boulders. Then Pembe and Boma pushed against the boulders as Mufasa directed them. The boulders started to rock.

"We must make sure the boulders fall when most of the ants are in the river," said Mufasa.

Zazu flew to the top of the falls. "Now!" he yelled.

"Push!" shouted Mufasa.

Pembe and Boma pressed their powerful shoulders against the boulders. Muwa, Pudini, and Nzee kicked at the last remaining rocks underneath. At last, the boulders rolled over the falls and crashed into the river.

Like a tidal wave, the river gushed over the falls with a tremendous roar into the water below. The wave swept away everything in its path, including the ants. Water rose over the banks like an enormous blue snake. It flooded the forest, swallowing the ants still on the land in a roaring cascade of foaming water.

Mufasa and his group cheered and jumped for joy. The Pride Lands were saved. So were many lives.

"So then what happened?" asked Kopa.

"Mufasa and the others congratulated one another on their success in saving the

Pride Lands. We cheered all the way back to Pride Rock," said Zazu.

"Was Mufasa still mad at you?" asked Kopa.

"No, he said he was delighted to have me as his trusted steward," said Zazu.

"And what about Sarabi and the other animals?" asked Kopa.

"Sarabi had taken all the animals to safety on the high plains. When we got to them, Mufasa called out, 'Sarabi, we have won!' A cheer went up as the word spread."

"Boy, they must have been glad to hear that!" said Kopa.

"Everyone was glad!" Zazu went on. "Sarabi came running up. 'Oh, Mufasa, we were all terrified that the ants would get you. I'm so glad you're safe,' she said."

"Weren't they proud of you too?" asked Kopa.

"They were. I flew overhead, and everyone cheered as I circled above. That was the most joyful moment I had ever known, my little prince. I truly felt like a hero."

"Did they ever find out what really happened with the false alarms?" asked Kopa.

"I'm about to tell you," said Zazu. "Mufasa made me feel as powerful as a Marshall eagle. He said, 'Zazu has kept us from danger! We must never doubt his word again.'"

"That's it?" said Kopa, wrinkling his nose.

"Not quite. You see, Nzuri, Lulu, Cheka, Sukari, Pamba, and Mayai, the young ones who tried to discredit me, felt so guilty, they confessed to Mufasa. He was furious but fair. He told the adult animals that the young ones had something to tell them.

"The young ones were ashamed and hung their heads while Nzuri explained how they were angry with Zazu for spoiling their fun. But they realized now how dangerous it was to try to discredit someone, especially someone who had the job of watching out for their safety. Their parents were so angry with their children, they wanted to punish them severely.

"But Mufasa was wise. He said, 'As your punishment, I command you, Nzuri, Sukari, Lulu, Cheka, Pamba and Mayai, to help Zazu gather news about all the important events in the Pride Lands. That way, you will learn the difference between fact and story—and you will also be held responsible for everything you say.'"

Kopa grinned. "That's why Rafiki always says, 'When the mouth is bigger than the brain, the feet won't stay on the path.'"

"And that's not all he says," added Zazu. "He also says, 'If the coconut bounces too high when it falls from the tree, don't eat it.'"

"I get it." Kopa giggled. "If

something doesn't seem right, then it's probably wrong."

"Precisely," said Zazu. "Check your facts!"